Big Pigs

Leslie Helakoski

BOYDS MILLS PRESS

AN IMPRINT OF HIGHLIGHTS

Honesdale, Pennsylvania

Boyds Mills Press
An Imprint of Highlights
815 Church Street
Honesdale, Pennsylvania 18431

Printed in China
ISBN: 978-1-62091-023-8
Library of Congress Control Number: 2013947713

First edition
The text of this book is set in Lemonade.
The illustrations are done in acrylic.
10 9 8 7 6 5 4 3 2 1

For Connor, with love until slop freezes over

Three piglets ran into the farmyard.
"Be good little pigs," called Mama Pig from the barn door.

"Humph!"

snorted the piglets. "We're not little."

Sweet Pea eyed his brothers and said,

"First one to sneak into the garden is a **big pig**."

Shush.

The piglets squeezed through
the fence as quietly as they could.
They scraped and scrambled.
They squiggled and jiggled.
They shoved and shimmied.

Until . . .

Sweet Pea popped into the garden and said . . .
"I'm a big pig,
no slow pokin'.
Sneaked in first.
This ham was smokin'."

"Humph!"

snorted the others.

Nibbles eyed the vegetables and said,

"First one to eat a whole row is a **bigger pig**."

Slop.

The piglets filled their snouts
with as much as they could.
They **gobbled** and **gulped**.
They **mashed** and **mangled**.
They **swallowed** and **swilled**.

Until . . .

Nibbles finished first and said . . .
"I'm a bigger pig,
greedy and rude.
Dug right in
and hogged the food."

"Humph!"

snorted the others.

Clean Bean eyed the mudhole and said,

"First one to sink in the mud is the **biggest pig!**"

Bloop.

The piglets sank in the mud as low as they could.
They **flopped** and **plopped**.
They **muddled** and **puddled**.
They **walloped** and **wallowed**.

Until . . .

Clean Bean sank the lowest and said . . .
"I'm the biggest pig,
dirty clean through.
I'm low down
and smell—pee-yoo!"

"Humph!"

snorted the others.

"You're not the biggest pig—I am!" said Sweet Pea.

"No, it's me!" said Nibbles.

"We'll see about that!" cried Clean Bean.

The piglets wrestled out of the mudhole . . .

over the garden . . .

through the fence . . .

and back into the farmyard.

They rumbled, bumbled, and tumbled until the shadows grew long and Mama Pig clomped into the yard.

"Humph!"

snorted Mama Pig.

"Are you the pigs who sneaked into the garden, ate all the food, and dragged half the mudhole into the yard?"

The piglets hung their heads and mumbled, "Yes, Mama."

"That's the sneakiest, greediest, dirtiest behavior
I've ever seen." Mama Pig shook her head, marched them
into the barn, and closed the door.

"I'm so proud I could bust a gut!"
Three piglets squealed and hugged Mama Pig tight.
Mama snuggled her piglets.
"Each of you is big in your own way, but . . .
whoever kisses me goodnight
will always be **my little pig**."

Smush. Smack. Smooch.

Sweet Pea, Nibbles, and Clean Bean kissed
Mama Pig as many times as they could.

Mama Pig tucked them into bed and whispered,
"First one to sleep is a lazy pig!"

Snort. Snore. Snooze.

Three **very big pigs** fell asleep as fast as they could.